For Uncle Chris

First published 2016 by Walker Books Ltd
87 Vauxhall Walk, London SE11 5HJ

This edition published 2019

2 4 6 8 10 9 7 5 3 1

Text and illustrations © 2016 Alex Milway

The right of Alex Milway to be identified as the author and illustrator
of this work has been asserted by him in accordance with the
Copyright, Designs and Patents Act 1988

This book has been typeset in Burbank Big Regular

Printed and bound by CPI Group (UK) Ltd, Croydon, CR0 4YY

British Library Cataloguing in Publication Data:
a catalogue record for this book is available from the British Library

ISBN 978-1-4063-7880-1

www.walker.co.uk

PIGSTICKS AND HAROLD

AND THE PIRATE TREASURE
AND THE

Alex Milway

WALKER
BOOKS

A New Pig in Town

One morning, Pigsticks was woken by a knock at his window. It was Harold.

"Wake up, Pigsticks!" he cried. "Tuptown's in trouble!"

"Come back after breakfast," mumbled Pigsticks.

"There's no time for breakfast!" said Harold.

Pigsticks threw on his dressing gown. He knew it must be serious - Harold never missed breakfast.

Harold dragged Pigsticks outside. "They're going

to destroy Tuptown!" he cried.

"Nonsense!" said Pigsticks. "No one would dare…"

But Pigsticks was wrong.

Tuptown was swarming with diggers. Workers were about to knock down the whole town - starting with Queen Pigtoria's Fountain.

"Stop!" cried Pigsticks. "You can't do this! Tuptown belongs to us!"

A mean-looking pig marched up to Pigsticks. "Actually," he snorted, "Tuptown belongs to me."

"So, we meet again, Sir Percival," said Pigsticks. Sir Percival Snout was a distant relative and he'd been a thorn in Pigsticks' trotter ever since they were piglets. At school, he always copied Pigsticks' homework. He even cheated in the three-trottered race at Sports Day.

"Queen Pigtoria gave this land to the people of Tuptown," said Pigsticks. "Everyone knows that!"

"Prove it!" growled Sir Percival.

"I can't," said Pigsticks. "The deed to Tuptown has been lost for generations."

"What – this, you mean?" said Sir Percival, holding out an old piece of paper. "It says here that I am the heir to Tuptown. This land is mine!"

Pigsticks looked at the deed. "Where's the queen's royal seal?" he said.

"It must have faded," said Sir Percival. "You have one day before I knock down your little houses and build a gold-plated mansion ... IN THE SHAPE OF MY HEAD!"

"If you really own Tuptown, let me buy it from you!" cried Pigsticks. "How does a million sound?"

"Not enough!" said Sir Percival. "I want two million."

"Two million is pocket money to a pig like me!"

"Then triple it! I want three million by midday tomorrow."

Pigsticks realized he'd got overexcited. But it was too late. "It's a deal," he said.

Back at home, Pigsticks was facing the facts: the only thing in his piggy bank was a hole.

"There must be a way to get the money," said Pigsticks. "Let's get our thinking caps on!"

Harold had forgotten his thinking cap. He started thinking without it, hoping Pigsticks wouldn't notice.

"We could set up a cake shop," said Harold.

"You'd eat all of our cakes before we could sell them," said Pigsticks. An idea hit him: "How about we put on a fundraising concert, starring me?"

The very thought of Pigsticks singing made Harold feel quite ill.

"What we need is to win the lottery, or find some buried treasure," said Harold.

"Harold, you're a genius!" cried Pigsticks. "There is a tale of long-lost treasure in my family. It belonged to my horrible great-great-grandpig, Pirate Pigbeard the Awesome!"

"You have a pirate grandpig?" said Harold.

"Sadly, you can't choose your family," said Pigsticks. "Pirate Pigbeard made a fortune in gold and jewels, which legend says he buried one dark and stormy night."

"I hope he had an umbrella," said Harold.

"Pirates are always prepared for rain," said Pigsticks. "But he wasn't prepared for the stampede of seahorses that killed him. Luckily he left this map behind with a riddle saying how to find his hidden treasure. No one has ever solved the riddle. If we can do that, we can find his fortune and save Tuptown!"

ABRAHAM-BONE LINCOLN

QUEEN PIGTORIA

PIGBEARD

CLEOPIGTRA

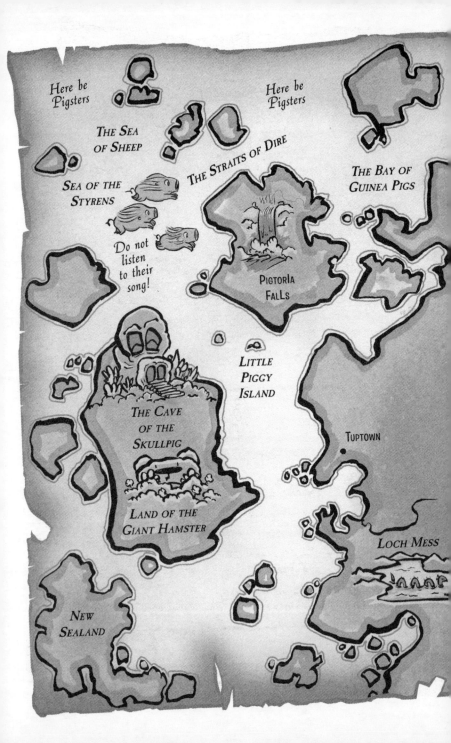

SEACOW COAST

THE HAMSTER PASS

TEMPLE OF THE TROTTER

MOUNTAINS OF MOO

THE ICE CREAM DESERT

Watch out!
This way
madness lies

HAMAZON JUNGLE
Beware! Deadly
crocodiles lurk

THE RIDDLE OF PIGBEARD'S TREASURE

On Little Piggy Island where
seabirds sing.

My treasure is guarded by claw
and wing.

Dig deep for a chest that
lies unseen,

To claim a prize that's fit
for a queen.

"That's a very difficult riddle," said Harold. "How will we ever solve it?"

"We must follow in Pigbeard's footsteps," said Pigsticks. "We must think like pirates, talk like pirates, walk like pirates ... we must BE pirates!"

"I don't want to be a pirate," said Harold.

"Of course you do!" said Pigsticks. "You'll make new friends...

Get lots of fresh sea air...

And travel to far-off lands!"

Harold watched nervously as Pigsticks laid out his pirate things. "Why don't you ask Pirate George to help instead?" he said. "He used to be a pirate captain!"

PIRATE GEAR

1. **SHIP IN A BOTTLE** For very small boating emergencies

2. **PIRATE HAT** For scary first impressions

3. **STINKY BOOTS** Perfect for dancing a hornpipe

4. **EYEPATCH** For scary second impressions

5. **VERY DEAD PARROT** Won't talk back

6. **SAILOR'S SHIRT** For lesser pirates

7. **TELESCOPE** For looking at things

8. **TREASURE CHEST** For stolen booty

9. **BANDANA** For looking dangerous while keeping the sun off

10. **JOLLY ROGER** Every ship needs one!

11. **PLANKS** For walking off

12. **GROG** Official nasty drink of pirates

13. **HOOK** For scratching a piratey itch

14. **PIRATE COAT** For pirate captains ONLY!

15. **CANNON** For firing at things

"I don't need another captain," said Pigsticks.
"I need a first mate, and that's you! Now, try on this
pirate hat and think of the sea…"

Suddenly, Harold felt much more like a pirate.

"Now, let's solve Pigbeard's riddle!" said Pigsticks.

"Aye aye, Captain," said Harold.

The first part seemed easy enough:

On Little Piggy Island where seabirds sing...

"We need to find Little Piggy Island," said Harold.

"And to do that, we need a ship."

"Let's go to Otterly's boatyard!" cried Pigsticks.

"Quick! We only have one day to save Tuptown!"

A Monstrous Discovery

O tterly showed Pigsticks and Harold her
fastest ship. "It's a jet-propelled speed boat,"
she said. "You just tell it where to go and it steers
itself. Ideal for the modern pirate in a hurry."

But Pigsticks had already seen the boat for him.

"That one's not safe to sail," said Otterly.
"It could sink at any moment ... and there's a big
storm coming!"

"Pirates aren't scared of storms," cried Pigsticks.
"Hoist the mainsail! Raise the umbrella!"

They set sail. But Otterly had been right – a
deadly storm was heading their way.

Pigsticks and Harold washed up on a sandy

island. Their ship was wrecked, and their pirate

gear was scattered all over the beach.

But then Pigsticks realized something. "Listen!

The birds are singing! Just like in the riddle:

On Little Piggy Island where seabirds sing..."

"We made it!" said Harold.

The seabirds crowded around them. One old, crusty-looking bird started to talk. "Who are you, and what are you doing on this 'ere island?" she said.

"None of your business," said Pigsticks. "Who are YOU?"

"They call me Seabird Bonnie," said the seabird, "'cause I'm a seabird. And my name is Bonnie. If I were you I'd turn back now. The island's full of danger..."

"What kind of danger?" asked Harold.

"There's a terrible monster up ahead with eyes as black as the night..."

Harold started to tremble.

"And claws as sharp as razor clams..."

Harold wanted to go home.

"And a beak as pointy as a cutlass!"

"Black eyes, claws and a beak?" said Pigsticks.
"It sounds like a bird to me."

"Oh, but it's not just any bird!" said the seabird.
"This 'ere bird is the size of a house, and as
fearsome as a shark. And its name is ... **ALAN**!"

"Alan?" said Pigsticks.

"Aye. **ALAN THE
ALMIGHTY ALBATROSS**.
You'll stay away,
if you know
what's good
for you!"

"No pig is scared of a bird," said Pigsticks.

"I think some hamsters are," said Harold. "Maybe I should just stay here..."

"Never!" said Pigsticks. "We need to go deeper into the island to find the treasure! Come on Harold, we're running out of time."

"You're right," said Harold.

"I'm always right," said Pigsticks. "Now, gather up our things, and let's go. Onwards!"

Harold picked up the most important things from the beach and set off after Pigsticks through a strange, rocky valley. It was so quiet that Harold could hear his own heart beating. Then –

SQWAAAAAARK!

"What was that?!" cried Harold.

Pigsticks quickly discovered what had made the terrifying noise. It didn't look very scary.

"It'll eat us for lunch!" cried Harold. "In one gulp!"

"Ah... I see it now," said Pigsticks.

"Of course you do!" said Harold. "It's enormous, and it's right in front of us."

"No!" said Pigsticks. "The riddle: My treasure is guarded by claw and wing. Alan is guarding the treasure. We'll have to defeat him if we want to save Tuptown! Pass me my cutlass."

But Harold hadn't picked up the cutlass from the beach. "I've got ... Battenburg cake?" he said.

"Brilliant!" cried Pigsticks. "Seagulls love other people's food! On the count of three, throw it!"

"We did it. And we're alive!" cried Harold.

"Of course we are," said Pigsticks. "And now for the next line of the riddle: Dig deep for a chest that lies unseen."

For the next hour, Harold dug deep holes all over the sandy valley, hoping to find the treasure. But they had no luck whatsoever.

Just as Harold was getting tired of digging and Pigsticks was getting tired of pointing at places to dig, Seabird Bonnie flew towards them.

"You aren't looking for buried treasure, by any chance?" she asked.

"Maybe we are, maybe we aren't," said Pigsticks.

"Well, if you are, it's right over there. X marks the spot, see?" said Seabird Bonnie.

There, right in front of them, was a huge X made of stones. "I knew that cross had to mean something," said Pigsticks. "What are you waiting for, Harold? Dig! We're almost out of time!"

Harold dug down deeper and deeper. His arms ached, his feet ached, even his nose ached. At last, when the hole was as deep as six hamsters, Harold hit something solid.

"What is it?" asked Pigsticks.

With one last burst of strength, Harold lifted the treasure chest and slid it out onto the ground.

"It's Pigbeard's treasure!" cried Pigsticks. "Open it, Harold, to claim a prize that's fit for a queen!"

Harold levered the chest open with his spade, and Pigsticks lifted the lid ... but the only thing inside it was an old lump of stone with a cross on top.

"There's no treasure after all!" cried Harold. "Tuptown is doomed! I knew I'd be a rubbish pirate."

"Pirate Pigbeard hasn't failed us yet!" said Pigsticks. "The riddle says the prize is *fit for a queen*. We just need to figure out how. In the meantime, let's get back to Tuptown before Sir Percival knocks down our houses!"

Harold was at a loss. "But how?" he said.

Seabird Bonnie stepped forward.

"You'll be needing a raft!" she said. "And me and my friends can help you make one. Many wings make light work, after all!"

When the raft was ready, Pigsticks and Harold waved goodbye and set off on the long journey home. As they sailed towards the sunset, Harold studied the riddle on their map. "How can this lump of rock be fit for a queen?" he said. "What if the riddle is just too hard for us?"

"We're Pigsticks and Harold!" said Pigsticks. "Nothing is too hard for us!"

Harold really hoped Pigsticks was right.

The Secret of the Stone

Pigsticks and Harold reached Tuptown just minutes before midday. Pigsticks marched towards Sir Percival with his snout held high, but Harold hung back, ashamed. He still hadn't worked out the last line of the riddle.

"Have you got the money?" said Sir Percival.

"Not yet!" said Pigsticks defiantly. "But we will!"

"No! You're too late," sneered Sir Percival.

"Diggers, start your engines!"

The words of the riddle went round and round in Harold's head. He'd never thought this hard about anything before.

"A prize that's fit for a queen..." muttered Harold. He looked at Queen Pigtoria's fountain. It looked just like the painting of the queen on Pigsticks' wall. But something was missing...

QUEEN PIGTORIA

Suddenly, everything clicked into place. "WAIT!" he shouted. "The treasure isn't just a lump of stone - it's Queen Pigtoria's orb! It really is fit for a queen!"

Harold rushed over to the fountain and placed the orb in Queen Pigtoria's empty hand.

Nothing happened.

"It was worth a try, Harold," sighed Pigsticks.

But then Queen Pigtoria's arm dropped like a lever, and a deep rumble came from the fountain...

The fountain sprayed glistening jewels of every colour into the sky, like a very expensive rainbow.

There was enough to buy Tuptown three times over.

"I always knew that Queen Pigtoria held the key to the riddle!" cried Pigsticks.

But Sir Percival Snout laughed a horrible laugh. "You seem to think all these jewels are yours," he said. "But I think you'll find that they're on my land, which makes them mine – ALL MINE!"

"You are one salty piece of crackling," muttered Pigsticks.

But Sir Percival was right. If he owned Tuptown, he owned the treasure, too.

"Collect up my jewels!" ordered Sir Percival. "And knock down this horrid little town!"

The diggers revved their engines.

Pigsticks was heartbroken. He'd come so close to saving Tuptown, but he'd failed. He screwed up the treasure map and threw it to the ground in a huff.

Harold was heartbroken, too, but that was no excuse for littering, so he bent down to pick up the treasure map. For the first time, he noticed something written on the back. The writing was faded, but he could still make out the words: *DEED TO TUPTOWN*. There, on the paper, was the royal seal of Queen Pigtoria herself.

DEED TO TUPTOWN

I, Queen Pigtoria, in the year 1892, declare that Tuptown officially belongs to all its people, and not just pigs of high breeding.

"Pigsticks?" he said. "The real deed to Tuptown is on the back of our treasure map! Sir Percival's deed must be fake!"

Pigsticks took the map from Harold. "Good grief! We had the deed all along!" he said. "I told you we'd save Tuptown! Stop the diggers! This document says Tuptown belongs to us!"

"You can keep your snotty little town!" said
Sir Percival Snout, filling his pockets with jewels.

"Put those back!" cried Pigsticks, puffing his
chest out. "In the name of Her Royal Highness
Queen Pigtoria, I command you to leave
Tuptown – forever!"

Everyone cheered as Sir Percival Snout squealed

off into the distance, his curly tail between his legs.

Milton Rhino, the Mayor of Tuptown, slapped

Pigsticks on the back. "Tuptown is saved, and it's all

thanks to you!" he cried. "Let's celebrate!"

"Aye aye, Captain!" said Pirate George. "It's time to ...

There was enough cake and pirate grog for everyone, and they danced jigs and sang sea shanties all night long.

"What shall we do with Tuptown's treasure?" asked Milton, as they all took turns walking the plank.

"Well," said Pigsticks, "I think I shall build myself a new house - a gold-plated mansion ... IN THE SHAPE OF MY HEAD! Isn't that an excellent idea?"